You know him as **POOL BOY**, the star of THAT viral video...

WAIT

FOR

IT...

LIVE IN THE STUDIO

Pixelated for your protection!

Origin story of iconic image told in full graphic detail here

Oh boy, did that ever **BLOW UP!**

HANGING OUT WITH **P⚪⚪L BOY**

Brought to you by MARVELOUS MARVIN

OVER 2.5 BILLION VIEWS

And still rising!

Things that ALSO blew up:
- science experiments
- a substitute teacher (figuratively)
- an entire school (literally).

As seen here.

... who was then dramatically rescued yesterday on the high seas in jaw-dropping scenes.

Also pants-dropping scenes!

After surviving:
· robot sharks
· holographic pirates
· a poo-throwing monkey
· and so much more.
As depicted in
lurid detail here.

What a week
it has been!

He made it through a manic
# MONDAY,

A TRULY TERRIBLE
# TUESDAY,

AND A WHACKY, WILD
# WEDNESDAY,

NOW WHAT'S IN STORE FOR ...

For all our readers around the world – you're the best!

First published in Great Britain in 2024 by Simon & Schuster UK Ltd

First published in Australia in 2023 by Scholastic Australia
An imprint of Scholastic Australia Pty Limited
PO Box 579 Gosford NSW 2250

3 5 7 9 10 8 6 4 2

Simon & Schuster UK Ltd
1st Floor, 222 Gray's Inn Road
London
WC1X 8HB

Simon & Schuster: Celebrating 100 Years of Publishing in 2024

www.simonandschuster.co.uk
www.simonandschuster.com.au
www.simonandschuster.co.in

Simon & Schuster India, New Delhi

A CIP catalogue record for this book is available from the British Library.

PB ISBN 978-1-3985-2200-8
eBook ISBN 978-1-3985-2201-5

Typeset in Adorkable, Harimau, Kiddish, Sugary Pancake and Zakka.

Printed and Bound in the UK using 100% Renewable Electricity
at CPI Group (UK) Ltd

MIX
Paper | Supporting
responsible forestry
FSC® C171272

EVA AMORES & MATT COSGROVE

...THURSDAY

Simon & Schuster

# LIGHTS.
# CAMERA.
# ACTION!

## 7:00 am

'WAKE UP!'

Oh, I'm awake. Don't worry about that. I'm WIDE awake. I've never been **more** awake in my whole life!

The upbeat intro theme song of the most-watched breakfast TV show in the world blares out in the studio . . .

**'WAKE UP, WAKE UP, WAKE UP!'**

I WISH I was asleep, snuggled up under my duvet, dreaming about nice things. Instead I'm living a **nightmare**.

'W . . . A . . . K . . . E . . . U . . . P!' the catchy ditty continues. No need to spell it out. I **AM** awake. Look at these EYES!

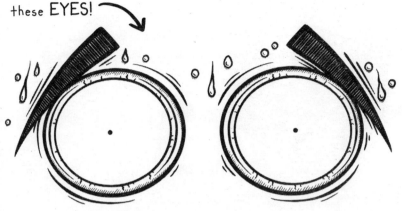

They are **132%** open. At least! (OK. Maths isn't my strong point. That has been established.*) And they are seeing EVERYTHING in **EXCRUCIATING** detail.

It feels like time is standing still and this terrible moment has been captured in SLOW MOTION, dragging out the pain as I notice every single, awful detail.

**'WAKE UP WITH KERRY AND PERRY!'** The tune hits its final, high-pitched note as the animated WAKE UP logo takes one last spin, ending with a cheeky wink.

*See *Worst Week Ever: Monday* page 81

All the monitors in the studio then cut from the smirking sun straight to an extreme close-up of **ME!**

I can't escape my FACE. In every direction, on every screen, there I am. Staring blankly ahead. Mouth gaping open.

I look like one of those CLOWN heads at the carnival.

The **circus** vibe is not helped by my unfortunate make-up situation or my clothing choice. Neither of which were my doing!

I think I got the WORK EXPERIENCE kid for my make-up **artist** before the show. My face looks like it was PAINTED by an **ANGRY** three year old!

And I use the term make-up 'artist' **LOOSELY**.
I know art is subjective, but seriously, I would have
preferred a **renaissance** moment instead of ABSTRACT
expressionism!

MORE LIKE THIS,

LESS LIKE THAT!

Draw me in
YOUR art style.

Don't get me started on this outfit either! The wardrobe department assured me it was straight off the RUNWAY.

*of AWE.

**of HORROR.

I actually want to run-AWAY, but I would probably trip over these ridiculous, baggy pants. Meanwhile, Marvin's make-up and clothes are PERFECT! He looks like he should be on the cover of a magazine. ➜

'Thanks for DROPPING IN to the **WAKE UP** couch, Pool Boy!' Kerry, the host, trills with a heavy emphasis on the word 'dropping'.

'Let's JUMP straight in the **DEEP END**,' her co-host, Perry, continues the cheesy, pool-themed word play, 'with the question the whole world wants answered. Exactly HOW did you end up with a major case of food poisoning, hanging off the edge of a ten-metre-high diving tower in front of your entire class, wearing nothing but rapidly disappearing crocheted trunks?'

Both hosts are smiling expectantly at me. Marvin is smiling smugly at me. I am surrounded by shiny, sparkling SMILES. I feel like I'm trapped in a toothpaste commercial.

No words are forming in my head. My lips aren't moving. No coherent sound, let alone an adequate answer, is emerging from my dry mouth. My brain appears to have gone on **holiday**.

The fixed **gaze** of the hosts are focused directly on me. Their eyes are **BULGING** wider and their smiles are getting impossibly **BIGGER** as they wait for me to reply. Soon they'll be nothing but **clenched** teeth in power suits.

Those teeth are giving me major robot shark
flashbacks ...

**ROBOT SHARK FLASHBACKS** ............................

... which is not helping my internal panic levels at all. I've
spun past all known levels straight to **CATATONIC STATE!**

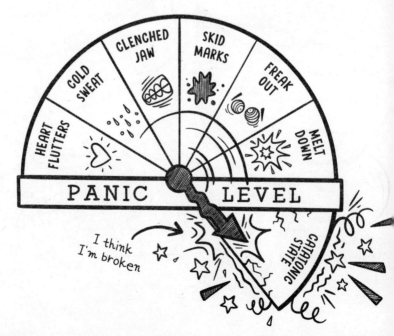

I think
I'm broken

I summon all my will to force my mouth **OPEN** and attempt to speak.

**What I WISH I'd said:**

'Reasonable question, my good fellow. [Chuckles conspiratorially.] I did inadvertently find myself in quite the predicament at the aquatic centre due to a calamatous, compounding sequence of extraordinary, unexpected events. Hard to believe 'twas only three short days ago but time certainly flies when you're an international internet sensation.'

**What I ACTUALLY say instead:**

'[Weird, guttural grunting.]'

Kerry and Perry's beaming smiles only **falter** for a split second, but it's long enough for me to glimpse their true reactions to my **BIZARRE** behaviour. Meanwhile, Marvin is loving it.

**FLUMMOXED**

**BAMBOOZLED**

**ELATED**
(No change in expression!)

I imagine all the audience watching my **BUMBLING,** **blundering** breakfast television debut. And they wouldn't have to be professional and polite about it like the hosts.

Yes. Even though it feels like hours, only one minute has passed

It seems like the cameras are all zooming in on me, CLOSER and **CLOSER!** Waiting for me to form real words.

The harsh studio lights are burning brighter and getting hotter. I'm both FROZEN and **MELTING** at the same time, like an **ice-cream** at the beach in summer.

I can't move but I can feel the sweat trickling down my face. My breathing is RAGGED. I can hear my heart **thumping** against my rib cage.

I'M NOT GOING TO MAKE IT!

THUD!

THUD!

THUD!

In fact, **EVERYONE** in the studio can hear my heartbeat. The sound technician taped a microphone to my chest earlier and the amplified

**THUD,
THUD,
THUD,**

is being broadcast live, like the angry footsteps of a **GIANT.** Which is freaking everyone out. Especially **ME!**

*Still smiling.
Just!*

The stress **SWEAT** is starting to pour out of me in **RIVERS** now. I look like I've just gone for a dip in the pool. And I can feel that tiny microphone slowly start **SLIDING** down the **slick** sheen of sweat on my skin.

The microphone should be **UP** here ...

Lousy, UN-sticky tape

... but it has slid **DOWN** here to belly button level.

# GURGLE! GRUMBLE!

Belly button lint. Don't judge me!

The **sloshing** sounds inside my churning stomach are shared at considerable **VOLUME** with the entire audience. I blame the combination of my nerves **AND** the complimentary muffin basket in the dressing room. (It would have been **RUDE** not to eat them. All.)

FLASHBACK

NOM NOM NOM

till sliding. Yikes!

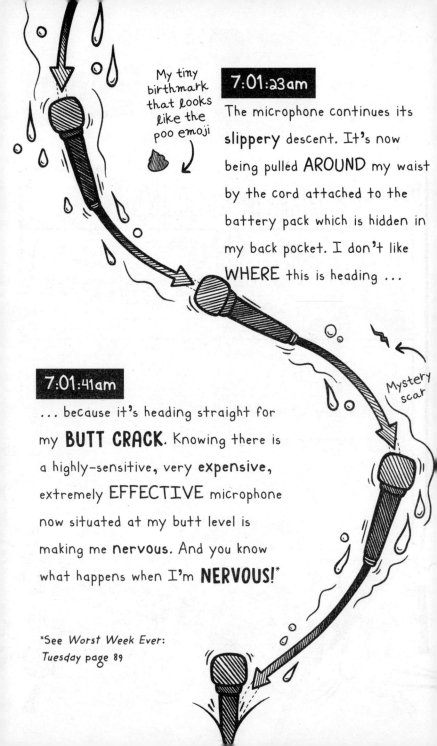

My tiny birthmark that looks like the poo emoji ↘

**7:01:23am**

The microphone continues its **slippery** descent. It's now being pulled **AROUND** my waist by the cord attached to the battery pack which is hidden in my back pocket. I don't like **WHERE** this is heading ...

Mystery scar

**7:01:41am**

... because it's heading straight for my **BUTT CRACK**. Knowing there is a highly-sensitive, very **expensive**, extremely **EFFECTIVE** microphone now situated at my butt level is making me **nervous**. And you know what happens when I'm **NERVOUS!**\*

\*See *Worst Week Ever: Tuesday* page 89

It's loud. It's amplified. It's captured in perfect clarity with impressive **BASS**. With the aid of the microphone I have blown away all previous flatulence sound levels.

It is the **FART** heard around the world, beamed into the homes, kitchens, lounge rooms, televisions, phones and eardrums of an unsuspecting globe.

Kerry and Perry are lost for words. I'm guessing this **fart-icular** situation WASN'T covered in Breakfast Television Host school.

That's it. Class dismissed.

STEP 1 SMILE    STEP 2 NOD    STEP 3 REPEAT

THE UNIVERSITY FOR TV PERSONALITIES

Marvin seizes this prolonged moment of **STUNNED** silence to PIPE UP and take over talking. And, boy, can he **talk**!

'In answer to your question, Perry, how did he end up on the diving board, well that was all **MY** brilliant idea. Then, as the brains and **TRUE** talent behind the video, I moved to the ideal position to capture the scene in all its **GLORIOUS** detail. The angles were just right as the action let rip. Speaking of RIPPED, Perry, have you been working out? Looking good! Anyway, back to my genius. It was the perfect shot. The lighting was **gorgeous**, as is that shade of your lipstick, Kerry. Now as a director realising my creative vision, I often have to work with those **MUCH** less talented than myself...'

While Marvin **PRATTLES** away I tune out and my eyes wander around the studio. Beyond the couch are a whole crew working hard to broadcast my **HUMILIATION** to the world. There's camera operators, sound technicians, people tapping on computer keyboards and others checking clipboards.

The producers are pacing back and forth making **important** decisions. Like this one:

Dad, Mum, Marjorie and Vlad are watching on from the side of the set, with very different expressions.

Dad is positively **beaming** with **PRIDE**. He's giving me an encouraging two-thumbs up. I bet if it was physically possible he'd be giving me two big **toes** up as well.

Dad is a long-time fan of a maximum-volume **FART** in the most **INAPPROPRIATE** places ...

Mum is **beaming** too. **LASER BEAMING** – with her eyes.

At me. At the hosts. At the producers. She does **NOT** approve and if we weren't currently **live-to-air,** Mum would definitely be sharing her thoughts.

I can tell she is compiling a mental list of topics that **WILL** be discussed in detail in the not too distant future.

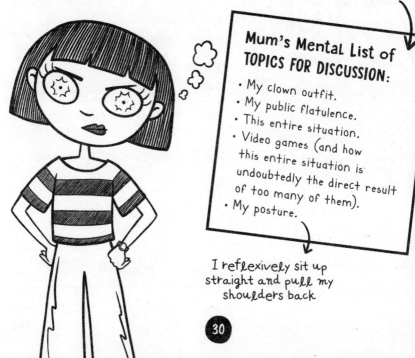

### Mum's Mental List of TOPICS FOR DISCUSSION:

- My clown outfit.
- My public flatulence.
- This entire situation.
- Video games (and how this entire situation is undoubtedly the direct result of too many of them).
- My posture.

I reflexively sit up straight and pull my shoulders back

Next to Dad is Marvin's Mum, Marjorie, AKA Ms King, my current principal and ... my future stepmum. **(EEWWWWWWWW! WHHHYYYYYYYYYYYY?)** She's nodding along happily, apparently **enchanted** by her son's never-ending monologue.

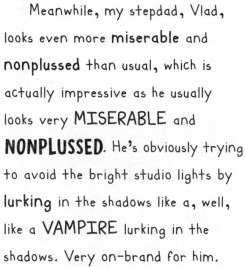

Meanwhile, my stepdad, Vlad, looks even more **miserable** and **nonplussed** than usual, which is actually impressive as he usually looks very **MISERABLE** and **NONPLUSSED**. He's obviously trying to avoid the bright studio lights by **lurking** in the shadows like a, well, like a **VAMPIRE** lurking in the shadows. Very on-brand for him.

If I was a vampire (like Vlad definitely is!), I would turn into a **BAT** right now and fly away.

Leaving in a flap

As Marvin has to pause to take a breath, Kerry quickly jumps in with another question, directed to **me** again.

'And Pool Boy, what do your parents think about all this international internet **INFAMY?**'

I stammer out 'My ... D ... d ... dad ...' partly because my brain is still on **VACATION** and partly because my dad has just unexpectedly **strutted** right onto the set.

He gives me a **WINK** as he takes centre stage. I am now afraid. Very **AFRAID.** The hosts look deeply **confused.**

'I can answer that one, Kerry. I'm **PROUD** of little Jussle Chussle here.' He ruffles my hair and I **wince** with embarrassment. 'So proud that I have officially changed the name of my business to ...'

I really, really hope that is just a **temporary** tattoo!
For Dad's sake. It won't age gracefully!

Dad's **SUPER HERO** style reveal has not gone down
well with the **WAKE UP** team at all.

Dad pats his belly with a drum roll and announces
straight down the barrel of the camera: 'Poo Dad Plumbing
– for all your toilet troubles!'

Speaking the forbidden **POO** word out loud on breakfast
TV has triggered the producers to leap into action.

They both **storm** onto the set to grab Dad but he still has more to say in his unofficial commercial.

## 'CALL 1-2-FLUSH NOW! 3% OFF FOR THE FIRST 10 CALLERS! USE THE CODE WORD "POTTY".'

The producers are chasing Dad in circles around the couch now, like Captain Fluffykins chasing Nickers around the house.

The sight of my face JIGGLING all over Dad's stomach is unsettling yet **mesmerising** as he continues his couch laps.

'Cut to the NEWS!' the producers yell.

'Let's cross to Sana at the newsdesk for the latest news.' Perry smiles weakly on autopilot.

There goes some belly button lint

**7:05am**

## LIVE FROM THE NEWSDESK

Mysteriously, overnight the world-famous Sphinx got a mystery makeover with a mysterious feline facelift that has drawn massive, curious crowds. Authorities are baffled by the mystery.

Closer to home, unexplained sinkholes have been popping up across the country without explanation.

BEFORE

RIDDLE OF THE SPHINX REBOOT

AFTER

CAT-CHY NEW LOOK. WE AIN'T LION.

THAT SINKING FEELING

36

All we can currently confirm is that the sinkholes are in no way related to any activity from Steel Corporation.

STEEL CORP IS GOOD

NOTHING TO SEE HERE

In other news, there sure do seem to be a lot of cats everywhere at the moment. On the streets, rooftops, there's one here right now. Purr-culiar!

WAKE UP!

MEOW WOW, KITTY CITY

And finally, just your regular reminder that Sterling Steel, the owner of Steel Corporation and all it's subsidiaries, including Steel Television, is ... the coolest. Officially. Back to you on the couch.

STERLING STEEL IS THE COOLEST

WHO IS THE COOLEST? POLL RESULTS*

*Based on a survey of Steel Inc. employees asked directly by Sterling Steel himself

100% VOTED STERLING STEEL

STERLING STEEL TOPS TOP POLL

Back on the Dad-free couch, Kerry smiles at me. 'Now we have a very special **SURPRISE** for you, Pool Boy!'

I GULP. In my experience, surprises are **never** good.

'We are crossing live to Wally Valley, Pool Boy's hometown, to speak to some of the special people in his life. Let's introduce his grandmother ...'

This is **actually** a nice surprise!

'... joined by his next door neighbour, Mia ...'

A **REALLY** nice surprise. Some friendly faces!

'... who are currently in Pool Boy's bedroom.'

LIVE

THE HOPPY DOPPYS

THE HOPPY DOPPYS

INSIDE POOL BOY'S HOPPY DOPPY-THEMED BEDROOM

# NOOOOOOOOOOOOOOOOOOOO!

Not the **ENTIRE** world, but in particular Mia, seeing inside my bedroom, which I would very much like to remind everyone I did *not* decorate!

I can feel my whole face is now matching my ROSY cheeks.

'Well, that looks just like my son's bedroom,' Perry says.

I relax slightly.

'My two-year-old son's bedroom,' he clarifies.

I CRINGE.

'This is a **fascinating** insight into the psychological profile of an internet sensation. Tell us, Pool Boy's grandma, has he always been **OBSESSED** with the Hoppy Doppys?'

'Oh yes. It was always Doppy Hoppys this and Choppy Boppys that with our young **scallywag**. Wait. I've got my prized photo album right here. Let me show you.'

Nan keeps flicking lovingly through the pages.

'Compelling! That explains SO much,' Kerry nods.

It explains NOTHING. Irrelevant. That was ten years ago. OK. Maybe five. Whatever. A very long time! I fail to see the relevance. OBJECTION!

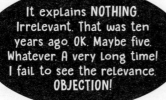

My lawyer impersonation!

'And is it true, Granny, you made those **WEIRD** crocheted trunks that completely **unravelled**?' Perry asks.

'I don't think I like your **TONE**, young man!'

'But you must admit crocheted trunks do sound a bit **STRANGE**. And impractical. And **scratchy**,' Perry presses.

'I'll show you impractical and scratchy!'

No-one criticises Nan's crocheting (or cooking!). No-one.

She unleashes with her walking stick and her finest swear words.

#@&*!!

BAM! BAM!

And seeing Nan **WHACKING** the camera ...

POOL BOY'S GRANDMOTHER ATTACKS

... Mia **shrugging** sheepishly the way she does ...

IMPRESSIVE SWING FOR A GRANNY

... and my boxes of missing belongings **finally** found, I feel a **LITTLE** better.

HOPE THIS IS COVERED BY INSURANCE

No Nickers. Drop my trophy!

'Um, let's leave that for now,' Perry says, a little shaken, 'and cross live to our next **SURPRISE** guest.'

Not **another** surprise!

Kerry takes over the introduction. 'We have another Wake Up **EXCLUSIVE** for you this morning!'

A disconcertingly familiar **silhouette** pops up on-screen.

'On the condition of absolute anonymity, an innocent eye-witness to the whole Pool Boy saga has bravely stepped forward to dish the **DIRT!** They promise to reveal the whole **SHOCKING TRUTH** ... right after this commercial break.'

# COMMERCIAL BREAK

Arty black and white photography

(Electric guitar riff)

VOICEOVER
(whispered):

Justin.

Chase.

Justin Chase.

Sweat.

Justin.

Sweat.

Chase.

Sweat.

Justin Chase Sweat.

SWEAT.

JUSTINCHASESWEAT.

The new fragrance from
Justin Chase.

SWEAT.

Each hand-crafted* bottle
of SWEAT contains a
single tear from Justin
Chase** that he shed while
thinking just of you.***

Smell the sweat.

Justin. Chase. Sweat.

Get Sweat. Available now.

\* Mass-produced.
\*\* Or someone else.
\*\*\* Or someone else.

While the commercials play, it is a **FLURRY** of activity on set. The producers are shouting directions at the crew. The hair and make-up team are frantically **PRIMPING** the hosts, whose smiles **vanished** the second the cameras stopped rolling.

I'm relieved when the **ON AIR** sign lights up again.

Until I remember what's waiting for me. **THIS!**

SECRET SOURCE SET TO SPILL THE POOL BOY SPICE

GULP!

'And we're back!' Kerry trills brightly. The smiles are back too. As fake as Nan's teeth! 'With our anonymous informant ready to lift the lid on the Pool Boy phenomenon.'

'Tell us **EVERYTHING** you know,' Perry implores.

The silhouette on screen begins GESTICULATING wildly. But there is no sound. **Phew!** I'm spared for now.

TECHNOLOGY, EH? THERE'S ALWAYS SOMETHING

'I think you might be on mute. Try unmuting!' Kerry suggests.

The mystery figure is pressing buttons. The suspense is **AGONISING**.

LIVE

CLICK!

NO LONGER VERY ANONYMOUS EYE WITNESS

That wasn't the unmute button. And that is **definitely** my teacher Mr Majors, who realises he is quite VISIBLE.

# NOOOOOOOOOO!

← I can lip read this

And even though he's still on mute there is no doubt that he is reaching serious **VOLUME** as he ducks under the desk.

UM, WE CAN STILL SEE YOU

The camera cuts back to the hosts, who try to smooth things over. After a nod from the producers, Perry loudly announces, 'I think it's time to ...'

# FACE THE PIE!

It's Wake Up's hugely popular **QUIZ** segment where guests must answer pie-related questions correctly or cop a face full of **PIE**. And Marvin and I are now in the **hot seats**.

7:15 am

I hope I get an easy question

49

'Marvin. Your question first. Can you name a type of pie that can be made from apples?'

'Can I have some thinking music, please, Perry?' Marvin drags out his time **unbearably** before finally answering, 'Is it ... apple pie?'

'Correct! You're safe from facing the pie!' Kerry cheers.

'Now, Pool Boy. Your question. What is the numerical value of Pi to twelve decimal places?'

### 'WHAT?!'

'I'm afraid that's incorrect. Now it's time to ...'

Everyone in the studio starts chanting **'FACE THE PIE!'** as the pie is LAUNCHED straight at my face.

As I wipe the cream filling out of my eyes, I see Mum looking extra-disappointed in me. I know **exactly** what she is thinking!

Another segment. **Another** surprise guest. We are actually, for real, I'm not imagining it, joined on the couch by extreme adventurer **WOLF GRUNTZ**. I don't believe it.

It's a little squishy

IBBIT RIBBIT

Neither does Mum! She might be Wolf's biggest fan!

WOOO!

Kerry ignores Mum and starts talking. 'It's a big **WAKE UP** welcome to our next special guest, Wolf Gruntz, here to give his unique perspective on Pool Boy and Marvin's jungle island ordeal **AND** to promote his new picture book.'

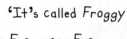

'It's called *Froggy the Frog goes Frog*. It's about a frog.' Wolf holds his book up to the camera.

'Which reminds me, I've also written a children's book.' Kerry holds up her book.

'I've written a picture book as well,' Perry joins in.

'Me too!' shouts Dad, running back onto the set before the producers grab him again.

Prototype only

What's **YOUR** great idea for a kids' book? Add it here.

There's **commotion** as Dad is dragged out of the studio by burly security guards. Marjorie runs after them **SQUAWKING**. Ever the professionals, the hosts get on with the interview.

'What **inspired** you to write the book, Wolf?' Kerry asks.

'The idea came to me when I was **trapped** in the **JUNGLE** facing certain **death**. As I was drinking my own urine to survive, I looked over and saw ... a **FROG**.'

'Well, I'm sure children will love that heart-warming tale,' Perry stammers.

'And then ... I **ate** the frog,' Wolf adds.

'That's a plot twist,' Kerry smiles nervously.

'I brought along some frogs to show everyone,' Wolf announces, reaching into the container he's been hugging. He pulls out a **massive** frog. 'Don't eat him,' he says directly to me.

Mum is **SCREAMING** again. Not in an **ecstatic** I-can't-believe-I'm-in-the-same-room-as-Wolf-Gruntz way anymore. Now it's an I'm-irrationally-terrified-of-frogs-don't-let-it-touch-me-please-**EWWWW**-slimy-yuck-GROSS ear-piercing SHRIEK.

Mum **FAINTS** but luckily Vlad's super quick (vampire-like!) reflexes means he catches her. She's **TOUGH** – just not around frogs – so I know she'll be fine. I watch on as Vlad carries Mum out of the studio.

So now it's just me and Marvin. And Wolf. **AND** the frog he's patting like a cat while whispering almost inaudibly, 'I love you, Froggy.'

'I think there might be a few more SCREAMS for our next guest, Kerry.'

'I think you might be right for **once**, Perry. Here to perform his latest hit single, please welcome to **WAKE UP** the **one** and ONLY Justin Chase!'

The floor of the set slowly opens and up rises Teen Heartthrob Extraordinaire (T.H.E.) Justin Chase in a cloud of dry ice. What an entrance! He is so unbelievably **COOL!**

'Hey, Kerry, Perry. Always a pleasure!' Justin fist bumps the hosts. Then he pivots to our couch.

'Wolf-man!' (Fist bump.)

'Froggy-dog.' (Pinky bump.)

T.H.E. Justin Chase pauses when he gets to me.

'My BRO! You get more than just a fist bump!'

The smokey smoulder combined with the perky pout. Breathtaking!

55

Justin grabs me up off the couch. 'Let's do this!'

And **THIS** is what we do ...

**13** HIGH FIVE

**14** PALM SLAP

**15** BACK HAND

**16** HOOK ...

**17** AND TWIST

**18** PINKY LINK

**19** ELBOW BUMP

**20** UP HIGH

**21** DOWN LOW

**22** KNEE KNOCK

**23** ANKLE TAP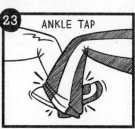

**24** ANKLE TAP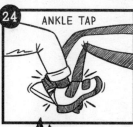

**25** BUM BUMP

**26** BUTT BUT

After witnessing the **PERFECT** execution of the secret JUSTIN CHASE handshake, Marvin's jaw hits the floor. He looks so **ENVIOUS** and **jealous** he is practically a plate of wobbly, green JELLY. This moment is absolutely **DELICIOUS!**

COLOUR
BY
NUMBER
1 = GREEN

**WHOOOOOOOOOOOOOOSSH!**

The floor

Marvin optimistically raises his hand towards T.H.E. Justin Chase, hoping for a fist bump, but is left **HANGING!**

This just gets BETTER!

'Bullies **aren't** cool, little man. Lift your game,' T.H.E. Justin Chase advises Marvin calmly.

Oh, yeah, did I forget to mention T.H.E. Justin Chase is my new **BFF*?!** How did that happen? I'm glad you asked.

I'll let my name twin fill you in ...

*Best Famous Friend

Have you ever had a bad week?

Maybe you had to wake up at 4:30am EVERY DAY to do an intensive EXERCISE regime.

73,231 ...
73,232 ...
73,233 ...

Maybe your personal chef/dietitian gave you green **SLUDGE** when all you wanted was PIZZA.

Green

Maybe your wardrobe stylist dressed you in really **RIDICULOUS** clothes you hated.

Maybe you spent every minute **REHEARSING** for tour or being interviewed and asked **exactly** the same question.

Maybe you had **PAPARAZZI** try to take photos of you going to the **TOILET**.

Called 'CHASERS' for a reason

Maybe you **snuck** out of your hotel room to get pizza but ended up being chased by **OBSESSED** fans.

Maybe you ran down a hotel corridor in **panic** but it was a **DEAD END** so you were about to get **MOBBED**.

And then maybe your bad week got a little better.

Maybe you KNOCKED on a random door in **desperation** and were actually **SAVED**.

Maybe your saviour was that cool little guy from the viral **MEME** who turns out to have the **exact SAME** name as you.

No way!

Maybe you hang out playing **video games** and talking all night and it's just such a **RELIEF** to find a friend and feel normal.

Cat videos

Maybe it's like you finally have the younger **brother** you've always **WANTED** but never had.

Maybe you come up with a fun, SECRET 'Justin Chase' ONLY handshake together before you head off.

# ⏩ FAST FORWARD

T.H.E. Justin Chase has now taken his position on the main stage. **Dramatically** the curtains behind him fall away to reveal a crowd of his fans, AKA **CHASERS,** outside the giant window.

The Chasers SURGE forward to the glass and go **WILD** when he starts singing his latest hit single, 'Thump'.

# THUMP by Justin Chase

Scenes from the video clip

Thump, thump, thump!
Thump, thump, thump!

That's my heart.
Off the chart.
It beats for you.
You know it's true.

Thump, thump, thump!
Thump, thump, thump!

Pumping blood.
You cause a flood.
In my arteries,
Veins and capillaries.

Thump, thump, thump!
Thump, thump, thump!
(Repeat to fade.)

Kerry and Perry have directed everyone on the couch to stand up and **DANCE** while T.H.E. Justin sings. Naturally, Marvin knows **all** the words (admittedly 80% of them are 'thump' so it's not that impressive), but he also has **ALL** the smooth moves.

I try to sit this one out with Wolf. He's not a dancer either. But Kerry and Perry are persistent and eventually drag me up off the couch.

I awkwardly try to move along to the beat and actually start to get into the **GROOVE** of the music. I notice the cameras zooming in on me again but I'm really caught up in the song. It is my good buddy up there performing after all!

Marvin tries to get in between me and the camera to show off his moves. And that's when our DANCE OFF ...

... becomes a **PANTS OFF!**

☐ Accidental? **OR**
☐ Totally, absolutely, definitely intentional?

You decide!

WARDROBE MALFUNCTION!

My **bum** is now being beamed around the world **AGAIN!**

LIVE

Lucky for pixers

THE CRACK IS BACK. THIS IS GETTING TO BE A HABIT!

I **STUMBLE** about in a panic with the billowing pants pooled around my ankles. And that's when I **KICK** over Wolf's container, **unleashing** all of the frogs!

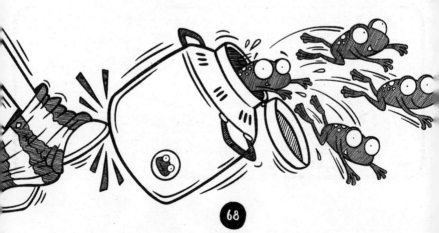

There are **hopping** frogs **hopping** every **hopping** where!

# SCENE DELETED

## BY THE CENSORS
(SO YOU DON'T LOSE YOUR BREAKFAST!)

Please enjoy these cute baby turtle pictures instead ...

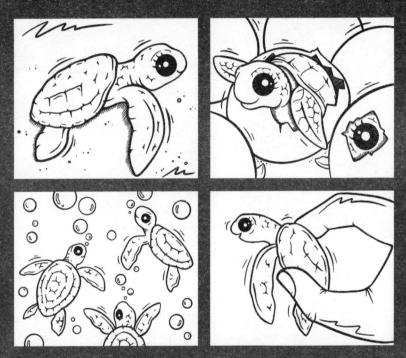

Apologies for the disruption to transmission.
We now resume our scheduled programming ...

**7:40 am**

I appear to have inadvertently **sprayed** Kerry, Perry, Wolf and Marvin with some of my frog-induced projectile **VOMIT**.

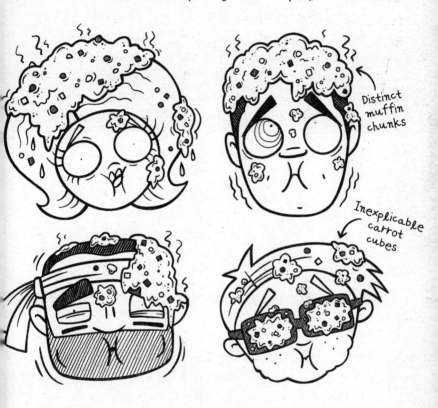

Distinct muffin chunks

Inexplicable carrot cubes

There is a brief, stunned calm before the **storm**. And then it begins. To the backing track of T.H.E. Justin Chase stoically continuing his song, three household-name celebrities and my arch-enemy unleash a tidal wave of **SPEW** ...

# SCENE DELETED

## BY THE CENSORS

(SO MUCH SPEW!)

Please enjoy these cute polar bear cub pictures instead ..

(Polar bear in snow storm)

(Still very CUTE. Trust me!)

Apologies for the disruption to transmission. We now resume our scheduled programming ..

The WAKE UP set is now the **THROW UP** set. Plus frogs.
It is **CHAOS!**

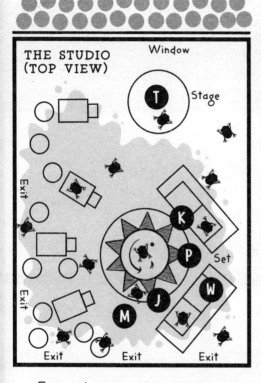

### KEY

**J** = ME!
**M** = Marvin
**W** = Wolf
**K** = Kerry
**P** = Perry
**T** = T.H.E. Justin Chase
(He's still singing.
True professional!)
🐸 = Frog
◯ = Wake Up Crew
⬤ = Chaser (x10)

**SPEW ZONE**

This area is increasing
exponentially as the
crew joins in the
pukeathon, all while
herding frogs AND
continuing to televise.

THE STUDIO
(TOP VIEW)

Window

Stage

Exit

Exit

Set

Exit    Exit    Exit

Everywhere people are
SPEWING and **SCREAMING.**
The producers look so MAD and
are using **swear words** I don't
think Nan even knows!

# SCENE DELETED

## BY THE CENSORS
### (FOR THE SAFETY OF YOUR OWN VOCABULARY!)

Please cover your ears and imagine these sounds instead ...

Apologies for the disruption to transmission.
We now resume our scheduled programming ...

**7:46am**

The MAYHEM is **ESCALATING** rapidly as everyone is ...

# SLIPPING    SLIDING    SKIDDING

across the slick, vomit-covered floor. And then there is ...

# SMASHING    CRASHING    CRACKING

as the studio is swifty, and thoroughly, DESTROYED.

Then a lighting rig falls and

# SHATTERS

GULP!

the giant glass window, meaning there is
now absolutely NOTHING separating all
those Chasers from T.H.E. Justin.

75

The Chasers flood into the studio, desperate to be closer to their idol. It is pure **PANDEMONIUM!**

To avoid the avalanche of obsessed fans, everyone in the studio bolts towards the emergency exits. It is a **STAMPEDE.**

THE STUDIO
(TOP VIEW)

I'm running breathlessly down an endless corridor of dressing room doors. When I see one with my name, I reflexively **dart** inside, **SLAMMING** the door shut behind me. I'm **SAFE!**

Or maybe **NOT!**

Stranger danger alert! Two very intimidating **HULKS**, dressed entirely in black, are slowly advancing towards me. And I don't think it's to give me a reassuring hug!

They're wearing dark sunglasses inside (one of Mum's pet hates) so it's hard to tell their expression, but they seem **CONFUSED.** They glance from the photo in their hand back to me over and over again, like they're doing a really tricky **SPOT THE DIFFERENCE.**

OPERATION:PP

TARGET

I don't want to be **GOT!** I reach for the only thing I can. A totally full basket of complimentary **MUFFINS**. And launch them like **GRENADES** at my approaching assailants.

**WHOOSSSHHH!**

Which does absolutely **NOTHING** to stop them. And then everything goes .

'So, Justin Chase ... we meet at last.'

I force my **heavy** eyelids open.
My **BLURRY** vision slowly comes into
focus on the face of some super-old
dude. He looks vaguely familiar.

Maybe he's from Nan's senior aqua aerobics class?

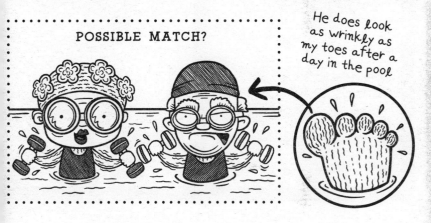

POSSIBLE MATCH?

He does look
as wrinkly as
my toes after a
day in the pool

I try to concentrate but it feels like my brain has gone
to another planet and in the empty VOID of my skull
someone is shaking **maracas**. My head **HURTS!**

ADIOS
MIGO!

RATTLE!
RATTLE!

81

I go to rub my forehead and realise my arms are **tied**. In fact, EVERYTHING is tied! I'm more trussed up than Captain Fluffykins after his catastrophic close call with Nan's basket of crochet wool.

KNOT GOOD MOMENTS

At least I'm not upside-down

'What's going on?' My head is throbbing. 'Who are you?'

'Who am I?' the old guy asks indignantly. 'Who am I?!' he repeats as if it is the most ridiculous thing he's ever heard 'Don't play games with me, young man!'

I can't imagine playing games with grumpy gramps. He looks like he cheats at Monopoly and flips the board if he loses. But right now the only game I'm playing is GUESS WHO?

He's **SQUINTING** at me hard through his thick glasses.

I'm squinting right back, trying to place his face.

IT'S A SQUINT OFF

Thicker than Nan's glasses!

'I'm sorry. I have no idea who you are,' I stammer.

'Don't you watch the news?'

'Um. Not really,' I confess.

The news is a bit **boring.**

Or DEPRESSING. Or **BOTH.**

I tend to tune out

whenever it's on the TV.

'Young people today!' he exclaims, and thrusts a business

card in front of my eyes.

Oohh, fancy, hard-to-read font. He must be important!

*Sterling Steel*

*Billionaire Extraordinaire*

*Owner & Founder of Steel Corporation*

*'It's good to Steel'*

'Still not ringing any bells. Sorry,' I apologise.

'I am the one and **ONLY** Sterling Steel! I own everything, everywhere and EVERYONE! I am the most powerful, influential and **FAMOUS** person on the planet!' he angrily proclaims.

'Justin Chase is definitely more famous than you,' I scoff under my breath.

'You refer to yourself in the third person?!' he fumes.

I look around. There's only two of us in the room so I don't know who this third person is.

'Enough of your **INSOLENCE!**' he splutters. 'I invited you here to my high-security, luxury mansion nicely, offered you a handsome fee to perform at my dear daughter's birthday party and you REFUSED. But no-one says no to Sterling Steel. **I GET WHAT I WANT!**'

He sounds like a toddler in the chocolate aisle at the supermarket chucking a TANTRUM.

I begin to understand what's happening here and try my best to explain ...

What I WISH I'd said:

'Oh, goodness, this is a pickle! It appears that we have a classic case of mistaken identity, which is interestingly also quite a common plot device in literature. In an almost Shakespearean twist of highly improbable coincidences, your intimidating hench-persons have regrettably abducted the wrong Justin Chase. Now, sir, I implore you to release me at once.'

What I ACTUALLY say instead:

'Me no Justin Chase.'

'I will not tolerate this **IMPERTINENCE!**' he bellows.

'You've got the wrong guy. I'm not Justin Chase!'

'Enough of this treachery and **DECEIT!**' he spits.

'I am not **THE** Justin Chase. I'm not lying!'

'We'll see about that.' He clicks his fingers and my kidnappers suddenly appear, flanking him on either side.

'Yes, Boss?'

'Bring in the ...'

The only lie-detector test I've faced before has been
Mum's single raised eyebrow. And I always failed **miserably**.

I'm **sweating** hard as the questioning begins.

'Are you Justin Chase?'

'No ... Yes ... Technically ... Wait ... Yeah ... Nah ...
It's **COMPLICATED!**'

'Yes or no answers **ONLY!**' Mr Steel orders sternly,
and repeats the question. 'Are you Justin Chase?'

I need to get out of this mess so I try saying 'No.'

'No more **LIES!** Is your name Justin Chase?' he shouts.

'Yes ... but...'

'Then it is settled! You, **JUSTIN CHASE,** will now make my darling daughter's birthday the best birthday **EVER!** Unless you fancy taking a **swim** in ...' (he pauses dramatically and clicks a remote control which makes the wall behind him slowly slide away to reveal ...) 'my **PIRANHA TANK!**'

I **don't** fancy taking a swim in his piranha tank. I'm still mildly traumatised by the Dude vs Death **piranha** episode.

I'm not about to be some fishy's **chicken dinner** if I can help it.

'Bring on the birthday party!' I smile weakly.

'That's more like it.'

Mr Steel plucks a list from his pocket and gives it to me. I nervously scan the DEMANDS.

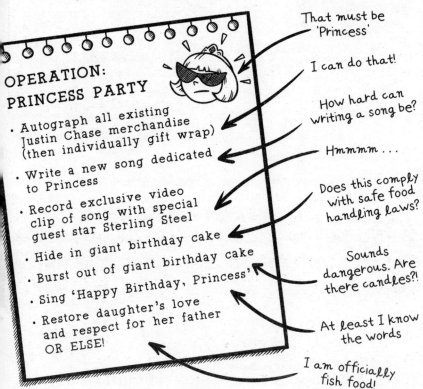

OPERATION: PRINCESS PARTY

- Autograph all existing Justin Chase merchandise (then individually gift wrap)
- Write a new song dedicated to Princess
- Record exclusive video clip of song with special guest star Sterling Steel
- Hide in giant birthday cake
- Burst out of giant birthday cake
- Sing 'Happy Birthday, Princess'
- Restore daughter's love and respect for her father OR ELSE!

That must be 'Princess'

I can do that!

How hard can writing a song be?

Hmmmm ...

Does this comply with safe food handling laws?

Sounds dangerous. Are there candles?!

At least I know the words

I am officially fish food!

'My **PRINCESS** has had a rough time of it lately and this **surprise** party will be the perfect pick-me-up. I want her to look at me again the way she did when she was my sweet, little baby girl.'

## THEN: & NOW:

'Well, enough reminiscing. Time is money! For me. Not you. Get **CRACKING** on that list. My daughter, for reasons I **FAIL** to fathom, is your number one fan, so you better not disappoint, Justin Chase. Or you'll be in **DEEP WATER!**' Mr Steel says gravely, pointing at the tank as he exits the room.

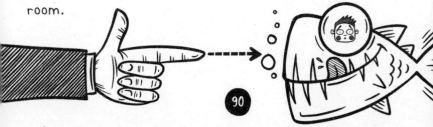

Signing time. I'm autographing as fast as I can, but there is so much Justin Chase **MERCH**! My signature has gone from

THIS

*Justin Chase*

to THIS

I honestly can't believe half of this **STUFF** even exists!

I'M CUCKOO CUCKOO FOR YOU

Justin time cuckoo clock

YUMMY

Justin Chase dinner set

Justin Chase case

Justin Chase toaster

JUSTIN CHASE'S BIG BOOK OF KNOCK KNOCK KNOCK JOKES

WHERE'S JUSTIN?

Justin Chase books

Ahoy there, me hearties. I dig you a lot.

SeA grEetiNg oRgan. I wiLL bUry yOu muCh.

Pirate Rap Justin official doll

Pirated Rap Justin unofficial doll

Justin Chase 2-in-1 shampoo & conditioner

Justin Chase bath bomb

Justin Chase fan for fans

**10:43am**

Phew. I've finally signed everything.

WAIT! How can there be **MORE?!**

**11:02am**

OK. **NOW** I've actually signed everything.

This is

**IMPOSSIBLE!**

**11:47am**

There's surely nothing else Justin Chase-themed on the planet
left to autograph. Now it's time to **WRAP** all the presents.
I just need to find the edge of the sticky tape first!

**11:53am**

I've found the edge of the tape!

**11:53:13am**

I've lost the edge of the tape!

Mission
impossible!

**11:59am**

I've found the edge of the tape. I really do try my best with
the wrapping, but I'm not sure this is where my talent lies.

## IN THEORY

## IN REALITY

How are
you meant
to wrap
a cuckoo
clock?

One down. Only 1327 presents left to go!
And I've lost the tape edge **AGAIN!**

Now I'm struggling to write a **catchy** pop song with nothing but a rhyming dictionary and the name **'PRINCESS'** to guide me. I have a new-found respect for T.H.E. Justin Chase. This song writing **CAPER** is harder than it looks! I try to make it as lovey-dovey as possible. After **multiple** failed attempts, I end up here.

Rejects

I'm under duress
And feeling the stress
Trying to impress
A girl called Princess... ✗

I would probably
wince less
If more words rhymed
with 'princess'... ✗

My fairytale princess
Locked up in distress
Gonna save you from disaster
And live happily ever after ✗

PRINCESSED
by a Justin Chase ✓

I've been Princessed.

You are the best.

And ever since

Wanna be your prince.

Or maybe your king

Has a better ring,

But then you'd be my queen.

You know what I mean.

Queen of my heart,

Never wanna be apart.

I've been Princessed.

Now I'm obsessed!

## SELECTED SCENES

**1:30pm**

This is **SURREAL**. I'm recording a **video clip** to the song I just wrote. It's amazing what you can do with a green screen! Mr Steel has ducked out of a business meeting to make a few 'COOL' cameo appearances. He's a bit of a **DIVA!**

I'm inside a giant cake.

**2:30pm**

I'm outside a giant cake.

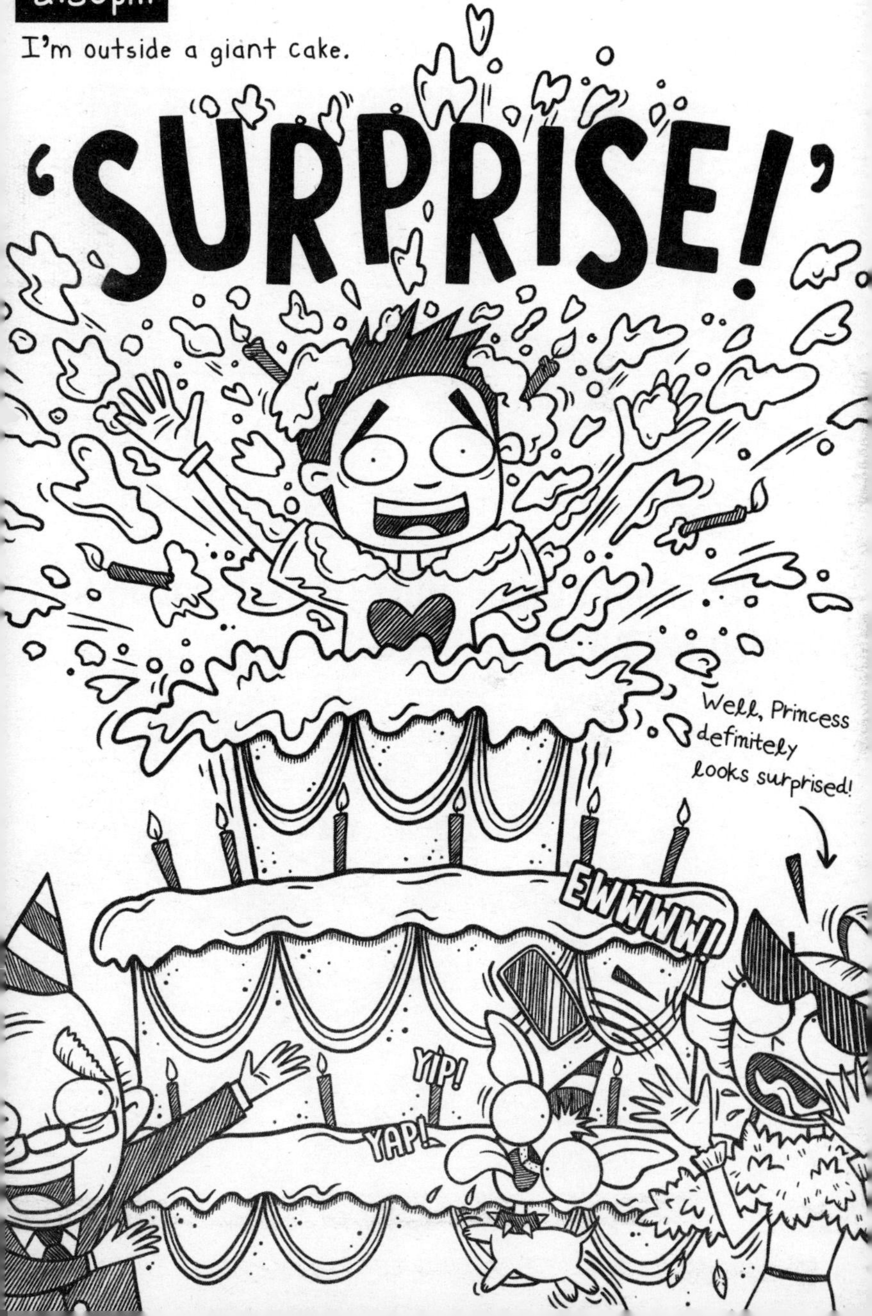

'EWWWW! DADDY! I ASKED FOR JUSTIN CHASE! THAT'S POO BOY! HE'S GROSS!

'UUUURGGGGGGHHH! MUMMY! TELL DADDY HE'S RUINED MY BIRTHDAY!' Princess wails.

'No, Princess. That **IS** Justin Chase. He wrote a song specially for you. We made a **COOL** video clip too. Let's watch it. I **am** cool. **PLEASE**, Princess!' Mr Steel hits play on his remote control and our video starts playing on a big screen.

A bit too much smoke!

CGI break dancing

'EWWWW! MAKE IT STOP! THAT IS NOT COOL AT ALL! THIS IS THE WORST BIRTHDAY EVER! FIRSTLY, NO-ONE EVEN CAME TO MY PARTY ...'

X-RAY VIEW BENEATH THE SUNGLASSES

Silent tear

'... AND THEN MY OWN FATHER, WHO CLAIMS TO BE THE MOST POWERFUL MAN IN THE WORLD, CAN'T EVEN GET JUSTIN CHASE TO TURN UP ON MY SPECIAL DAY. I'M HUMILIATED! I CAN NEVER LEAVE THE MANSION AGAIN!'

**2:30-2:45pm**

'WAAAH!'

**2:46pm**

Princess picks herself up from the floor and sniffles,

**'ONLY BRUTUS LOVES ME!'**

Mummy loves you too, sweetie!

I've been watching on silently in shocked **AWE** from the cake this whole time, too terrified to move. (But not too terrified to try the cake. Vanilla sponge. Mmmmm.)

Princess seems to have regained her composure. The screaming has stopped, but I'm even more scared now. As she slowly and purposefully walks towards her father, I can see ...

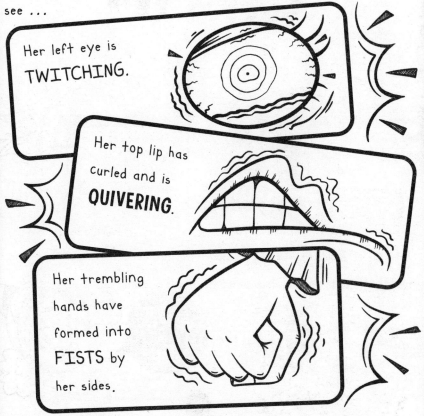

Her left eye is **TWITCHING**.

Her top lip has curled and is **QUIVERING**.

Her trembling hands have formed into **FISTS** by her sides.

'It's **happening**, Daddy,' she states calmly.

'No, Princess. Breathe! I'm **sorry**! Please!!' Mr Steel begs.

'It's too **LATE**,' she explains matter-of-factly as she casually reaches out her arm and **flicks** a vase off a nearby pedestal. All while maintaining defiant eye-contact with her father – just like Captain Fluffykins does with me whenever he intentionally **BREAKS** something at home!

## COMPARE THE PAIR

Priceless antique vase

SMASH!

My favourite glass (water just tasted better in it!)

SMASH!

Next Princess grabs a giant handful of birthday cake and **SMEARS** it across the pristine, white wall.

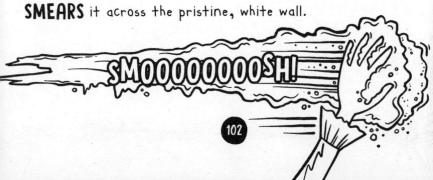

SMOOOOOOOOSH!

I don't believe it! If my mum saw that there would be oh so much **TROUBLE** right now.

Full laser eyes PLUS verbal tirade!

But no-one here is stopping Princess in her **RAMPAGE**, as she continues **throwing** cake and **BREAKING** things.

Daddy's little Princess, please calm down!

Mummy's going to take a nap now, sweetie!

I ain't cleaning that mess up!

That's a waste of good cake!

Princess has now moved on to the towering pile of presents and is tearing them apart in her terrorising **TANTRUM**, creating the perfect **DIVERSION** I need to sneak off. I make my hasty **escape**.

Sounds like a pterodactyl

RAH! YIP! YIP! YIP!

## 2:52pm

Apparently this isn't going to be as easy as I thought. The mansion is a **MAZE** of corridors. I could sure use some help finding my way out ...

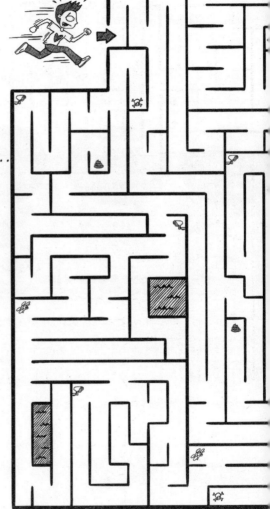

### KEY

 Security camera

 Surveillance drone

 Landmine from Brutus

 Dead end

 Indoor pool (or piranha tank – I don't want to find out!)

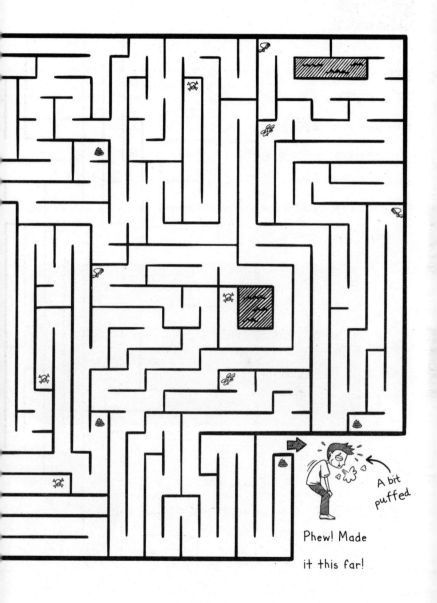

A bit puffed

Phew! Made it this far!

The door behind me **SLAMS** shut, and I appear to be
TRAPPED in a small room with no way out. The entrance
I came through is **locked** now. There are no other doors.
No windows. I'm feeling CLAUSTROPHOBIC!

My eyes dart around the room. One entire wall is just
a gallery of T.H.E. Justin Chase portraits. **WEIRD!**

On the opposite wall there's a small computer monitor.
I read the flashing message:

> ### FACE 2 FACE
> Stare and find the identical pair,
> Then press those two to change the view.
> We simply ask: complete the task
> Or this room will be your tomb!

I hear a **CLICK** and notice
there are now spikes slowly emerging
from the walls. YIKES! This
challenge has a time limit! I've got
to find the matching faces quick!

Answers on page 188

When I press the matching faces **ALL** the portraits **SPIN** around. This a two-part challenge! **WEIRDER!** The message on the monitor has updated:

Rearrange the panels to form the handsome face
Of International Recording Superstar
and Teen Heartthrob Justin Chase.
Then left to right the letters read
The secret codewords you now need.
Type them in, but hurry please,
Or you'll be turned into Swiss cheese!

I don't want to be a block of stinky **CHEESE**.

I frantically try to solve the puzzle as the pointy spikes inch ever closer. I think I've solved it and type in the code words.

Holey moley!

Could you crack it?

The floor drops away beneath me and I **PLUMMET** to the ground below.

FHOOOOOOOSSH!

I'm now in a **LABYRINTH** of MIRRORS. Everywhere I look, there I am – or at least a version of me.

Hanging from the ceiling is an envelope. I read the card inside:

> MIRROR, MIRROR,
> Which way to go?
> You'll never know.
> But the right direction
> Will be clear on reflection!

PLONK!

OUCH! But better than being turned into a human shish kebab!

I actually look like THE Justin here!

Printed on the back of the card is **GOBBLEDYGOOK** that makes no sense at all.

I try to find my way out of the mirror maze but it is endless **dead ends.** I just keep bumping into myself wherever I turn or whichever way I go. It is **EXASPERATING!**

PUTYOUR
HEADDOWN
ANDFOLLOW
YOURHEART

I read the clue over and over again, but still can't figure it out. I'm holding the card and staring at my **reflection,** disappointed, when suddenly it is obvious what I have to do.

Try reading the goobledygook in a mirror!

I look down and notice a tiny trail of hearts on the floor

They're pointing out a PATH. I follow the track and it leads me through the mirror **maze** to a familiar-looking, and very locked, heart-shaped **DOOR**. SO WEIRD! Billionaire mansion security is over the top!

I read the note pinned on the door.

FRONT

LET ME IN

BACK

Your exit is blocked
But the door can be unlocked.
Let the lyrics be your guide
To get to the other side.

What lyrics? There's no music playing. Then I remember where the door is from. It was featured in T.H.E. Justin Chase's video clip for his chart-topping, worldwide smash hit music single, 'LET ME IN'.

Marvin changed the lyrics to 'TOILET ME IN' to **TORMENT** me on Monday, but I know the real words. I think I understand what I have to do.

I **knock** on the door three times.

Nothing.

I **knock** three times again.

NOTHING.

I **knock** three times again.

Still **NOTHING**.

I notice there's a doorbell. Wow. I didn't see that before. I try the doorbell now.

The door remains locked. As my last hope I slide the note that says 'LET ME IN' under the door

I wait, in SUSPENSE, holding my breath. And then the unbearable silence is broken. I hear the jingling of **keys**. Right above my head. **LOTS** of keys. Too many keys! I look up ...

... it's raining keys! Now I just need to find the right one.
I bet it matches the key on the note. I start searching.

## 3:28pm

Once I've found the correct key I use it to unlock the door.
It swings open into an expansive room filled with nothing
but **SAND!** In every direction. There's no clue, but there
is a heart-shaped shovel with S.O.S. engraved on the handle.
As I scan the room again, I notice letters drawn into the
sand, and then I know where I need to start **digging**.

As I dig away I'm doing my best S.O.S. Pirate Rap. 'Ahoy there, me hearties. **X** marks the spot.' The shovel strikes something hard buried in the sand and then I start

SINKING...

CLINK!

... and I fall through the sand, landing in another room. This one is filled entirely with **SNOW!**

It is snowing. **INSIDE!** It looks like the setting of the video clip for T.H.E. Justin Chase's song 'COOL'. (I'm seeing a strong theme emerging here.)

A softer landing this time!

PLONK!

I trudge over to the cute, harmless-looking snow couple. One is holding a CLUE in his twiggy fingers.

### COOL

'I can be a ball, but I bounce not,
And I run away when it gets hot.'
This riddle you must now decode
Or my heart will soon explode.

I glance at the **love heart** on the snow-man's chest.

It is a literal ticking time **BOMB** with a screen counting down the seconds!

# PRESSURE!

I have to solve this **RIDDLE** fast. I read the clue again and look to the **snow**man for help, but get nothing. I feel like the solution must be staring me in the face, but it's **no** use. There's **no** answer popping into my head and the counter is ticking down. It's **now** or never!

The **answer** is right on the tip of my tongue but my brain is refusing to cooperate. And time is running out!

Snow

Dad's advice for problem-solving pops into my head:

Always think outside the box, Justo Chuzmeister!

I certainly need to get **OUTSIDE** this box before it blows up! I don't have the riddle answer but I do have a **SHOVEL!**

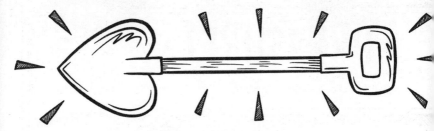

I look all around the **cavernous** room. There are no visible exits but I spy a possible weak point. The fake snow is blasting into the wintery wonderland from an **AIR VENT!**

It's up near the ceiling, but the snow underneath has piled high enough that I can just reach it. I use the shovel to **jimmy** the grill out and then I **CLAMBER** into the air vent, just as I hear a loud **BOOM** behind me.

`3:40pm`

I'm crawling as fast as I can through the tight tunnel.

CREAK!

The metal **GROANS** under my weight. And then it's too much. I fall through.

CREAK!

I don't think this is a Justin Chase pop song-themed room. This looks **SERIOUS!** The walls are lined with impressive hi-tech machines and **gadgets** I just can't resist touching.

Getting better at landing!

**INTRUDER ALERT!**

That's not good.

**LASERS ACTIVATED!**

That's **really** not good. One false move and I'm getting an extreme Mr Snipzy haircut ... or **WORSE!**

I'm trapped in the corner, unable to reach the conveniently labeled but inconveniently placed switch. It would take some advanced yoga skills to navigate those laser beams unscorched.

However, I do believe a **DRONE** might be able to make it through the lasers. I grab a remote control and give it a go.

I haven't operated a drone before but it's just like piloting the alien viking skeleton robot jet fighter in Manic Mayhem Battle Battalion Shoot Squad IX. Too easy!

After all that **practice** playing last night I'm able to MANOEUVRE the drone through the beams, **NO PROBLEM!** I wish Mum was here to witness this **historic** moment.

ANOTHER FANTASY SEQUENCE

I'd like to thank video games! I couldn't have done this without them.

I was wrong about video games all along. From this day forward you can play video games as often as you want!

LEGEND AWARDS

CLAP! CLAP! CLAP!

Standing ovation

The alarm and lasers have cut off but the only way out of the room is through this door, which is not very welcoming.

IDENTITY VERIFICATION

Voice recognition

Breath recognition

Fart recognition

PRIVATE

TRESPASSING PROHIBITED

NO ENTRY

GO AWAY

SCRAM!

Hair sample

Retina scan

Tongue scan

Belly button lint swab

Butt scan

Toenail clipping sample

NOT WELCOME

Maybe there's a key under the mat. I'll check, just in case.

**INTRUDER ALERT!**

There are no lasers this time, but the roof has started **lowering** towards me. I'm certain to be SQUASHED like a bug by a boot.

My new life as a **pancake** is about to begin when I hear ...

**YIP! YIP! YIP!**

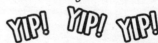

It's **BRUTUS** and a highly **improbable** dog flap! I squeeze through before I'm PULVERISED.

3:46pm

FOR APPROVAL

STEEL FOR PRIME MINISTER

STEEL FOR PRESIDENT

STEEL FOR KING

STEEL FOR WORLD LEADER

STEEL FOR INTERGALACTIC OVERLORD

TO DO LIST
• Operation PP
• Meetings
• Own everything
• Mine everything
• Takeover all media
• Takeover world
• Takeover universe
• Order takeaway for dinner

WORLD
MINE
LOG
DUMP
TRASH

SOLAR SYSTEM
MINE
COLONISE
DUMP
TRASH

A solitary high-backed chair, facing a wall of screens, begins to slowly **swivel** around towards me.

'... evil lair?' I suggest.

'No! My daddy's home office. It's so **tacky,** I know! But I wanted to watch you and this room has the best "views" in the whole mansion.'

'I don't understand!' I blurt out

'How do I explain this to a commoner?' Princess sighs.

Maybe your custom bedroom-wall **mural** of Justin Chase **STILL** isn't finished?

You can't rush genius

Maybe you went out for **brunch** and they cut your gourmet goat's cheese toastie in SQUARES when you **SPECIFICALLY ORDERED TRIANGLES?!**

Maybe someone filmed your perfectly **reasonable** response to substandard service and posted it online?

REC

Then maybe none of your **so-called-friends** turned up to your birthday party even though you had spent weeks preparing the most **EPIC** Justin Chase ESCAPE ROOM EXPERIENCE for them?

**Princess** PARTY TIME!

**Duchess** I'm busy.

**Countess** Can't make it.

**Camilla** Ewwwww!

**Priscilla** SOZ. Ur totes toxic now babe. LOL.

**Dramilla** As if.

**Urzilla** No way

Wait! Escape Room? There were SPIKES and BOMBS!

RUBBER spikes and GLITTER bombs! Perfectly harmless. Ergh! Stop being so melodramatic. And don't interrupt!

Then maybe your multi-billionaire father couldn't even get Justin Chase to come to your birthday party and then he **flies off** to some important business meeting just like he **ALWAYS DOES!**

# WAAAH!

**3:52pm**

I awkwardly try to console Princess. Her **sobbing** slows down as we start talking. We actually, somehow, seem to bond over weird dads and unwanted internet infamy.

'I suppose I should thank you,' Princess sniffs. 'Your **POO BOY** antics did push my **TOASTIE TRAGEDY** off the internet, after all. And now your gross **WAKE UP** appearance is blowing up **BIG** time. All those mean trolls have totally moved on from me. You're everywhere again.'

Princess starts to perk up as we look at the monitors. 'Anyway, you're so odd and icky, but I am willing to overlook that because YOU know **JUSTIN CHASE!** Tell me **everything!** What's his favourite colour? What does he smell like? What does it look like when the morning sun hits the barely perceptible dimple on his left cheek?'

Then Princess stops **swooning** and becomes deadly serious. 'Can you get me a meeting with **HIM?**'

I consider her request. 'Can **YOU** get me out of here and back home?'

## 3:53pm

On the condition of an introduction to T.H.E. Justin Chase, Princess is helping me **ESCAPE** the mansion. She easily navigates the maze of corridors, **dodging** security cameras and drones, but we still have to get past the **GOONS** who are blocking the exit.

... the GARAGE! Woah. Looks like I'll be making my getaway in **STYLE**.

Will it be the stretch limo with FLAMES and turbo **thrusters** or the all-terrain, jet-engine **MONSTER** truck?

4:29pm

... pull up outside home sweet home.

Ewww. Your house is old and creepy!

Nickers bounds out to greet me.

NICKERS! I'M SO HAPPY TO SEE YOU!

WOOF*
WOOF**
WOOF***
WOOF****

* You're back, small human.
** We saw you on the talking rectangle.
*** You taste like pie, frogs, sp and vanilla cake. Nice!
**** When are you going to introduce me to that little hur

138

Nickers and Brutus seem to be hitting it off with some serious **butt-sniffing**.

'Ewww. Brutus! Stop that! **GROSS!** You don't know where that dirty dog's been,' Princess shrieks in DISGUST. A judgemental but very valid point from Princess there.

She **snatches** Brutus away from Nickers and plonks her pampered pooch into the sidecar.

'I think we'll be **leaving,** but YOU owe me a meeting with **JUSTIN CHASE**. I know where you live now.' She **shudders** as she looks towards the house. 'And I'll be watching you. **ALWAYS WATCHING!**'

'Princess emphasises her words with some pointed gestures and then **roars** off on her scooter.'

Inside I find Nan busy crocheting and swearing. She's making something **BIG** with complicated stitches. As soon as she sees me, she drops her crochet hook and gives me a big **HUG**.

Did you get even taller?

I needed this hug

'Those **turkeys** at the TV show have finally finished with you? I'm glad you're home, Justin. There's a lot of **KERFUFFLE** happening here today. I better get back to work. Your father and his plans!' Nan sighs.

Dad bursts in on cue. I'm expecting this ...

Happy tears

MY BELOVED KIDNAPPED SON HAS RETURNED A LONG LAST! I WA DISTRAUGHT WIT CONCERN!

Instead I get **THIS** ...

RUFFLE
RUFFLE

Justo Chusto.
About time
buddy!

'Dad! Haven't you been **slightly** concerned that your only child has been **MISSING** since 7:49am?!' I huff.

'No point **complaining**, Judd Chudd. That's just the life of an **INTER-FAMOUS SUPER STAR**. And since you were such a **HIT** on the telly this morning ...' (Dad shows me his phone) '... you're probably going to be **tied up** a lot more in the future.'

POOL BOY MAKES AN IMPRESSIVE SPLASH. WAKE UP'S HIGHEST RATINGS EVER!

WATCHED BY MILLIONS AROUND THE WORLD

141

'Those nice TV producers from **WAKE UP** said they'd fly you straight home after us — as soon as you were finished your celebrity **DUTIES**,' Dad explains. 'They were **so** keen to get us out of the studio so you could concentrate on **IMPORTANT MEETINGS**. They're true professionals.'

'While you've been off having the time of your life as a **VIP** hot shot there's been a few exciting developments back here in the real world,' Dad continues.

'Last night, Marjorie and Marvo's house was swallowed by one of those **sink holes** that have been in the news lately.'

**BEFORE**                    **AFTER**      Maybe I should start watching the news

'I have a few **THEORIES** on the sinkholes.' Dad pauses dramatically to silently mouth the word '**ALIENS**', I'm assuming just in case any aliens are currently listening in on our conversation.

ÔŒØÖ*

*Dang. The hairy one is onto us!

'The important thing is M and M are safe and sound as we were all holed up in that **RITZY** hotel yesterday. Since Marjorie and Marvy don't have a home, they'll naturally be moving in **here** with us!'

Someone please hand me a glass. This is water-spitting level news.

SPLOOSH!

Dad isn't finished yet though. He continues exuberantly, 'And just to make it all TICKETYBOO, we've brought our **wedding** forward. To **TONIGHT!**'

This revelation requires two glasses of water. At least.

'You'll be my **best man** of course, Juz Chuz! That means you're in charge of the **RINGS**. I had them custom made! No expense spared. The Poo Dad Plumbing phone's been running **hot** since this morning. Business is **BOOMING** so I'm going all out for this wedding! And after tonight we'll all be one big, happy **family**. Me and Marjorie, husband and wife. You and Marvy, **BROTHERS!** Together **FOREVER!**'

FOREVER.

FOREVER!

FOREVER!

'And I've got one more awesome **SURPRISE** for you, Justickles!' Dad leads me upstairs to my bedroom. 'You're not just getting a brand new **brother**. You're getting ...

... a **ROOM MATE!**'

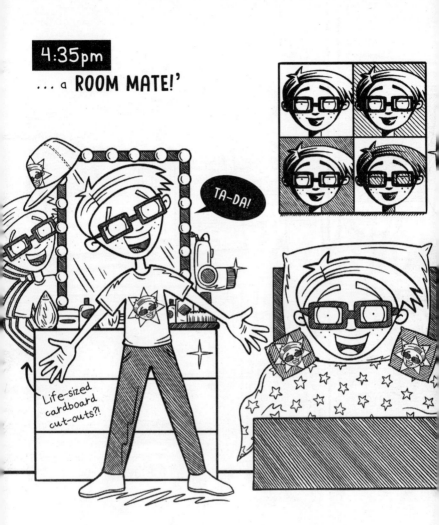

TA-DA!

Life-sized cardboard cut-outs?!

'I took the liberty of rearranging our room, Papa Harry. To be **extra** nice to my roomie, I gave Justin the windows.'

I find all of my stuff SHOVED over in the corner.

'Isn't that **SWEET** of Marvo, Junky Cheese?
Anyway, I've still got **lots** to organise for the wedding.
I'll leave you two **BROS** to catch up!' Dad disappears
down the stairs.

As soon as Dad is out of earshot the **real** Marvin emerges.

The mask comes off!

'I'm **NOT** happy about this temporary accommodation arrangement, Poo Boy,' he **sneers** at me.

'You better stay on **YOUR** side of the halfway line.' He points at the tape he's stuck across the floors and wall.

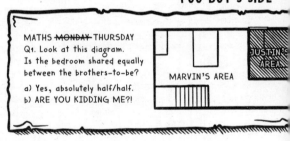

MARVIN'S SIDE

# DO NOT CROSS!

POO BOY'S SIDE

Even with my dubious maths skills I can tell the room **isn't** divided equally.

MATHS ~~MONDAY~~ THURSDAY
Q1. Look at this diagram. Is the bedroom shared equally between the brothers-to-be?
a) Yes, absolutely half/half.
b) ARE YOU KIDDING ME?!

JUSTIN'S AREA

MARVIN'S AREA

'Luckily, I store my Marvelous Marvin merchandise in a warehouse so it wasn't lost with our house. I've tried to inject some class into this hovel, but I'm warning you: **DON'T TOUCH MY STUFF!** Now I need to work on my channel since you tried to upstage me on TV this morning. My fans **need** me. So no noise while I'm recording **OR ELSE!**

Marvin gives me his best threatening **STINK EYE**, but he doesn't seem as INTIMIDATING now. I mean, I have faced poo-throwing monkeys, holographic pirates, sharks (both real and robotic), exploding snowmen, evil billionaires, piranhas, lasers (real), spikes (rubber) AND Princess after all.

SCARY

NOT SO
SCARY
ANYMORE

I plonk down on my bed and **RUMMAGE** through my pile of things. My missing boxes of belongings have been dumped there along with my stuff from the hotel.

I'm subtly checking if that strange **TALISMAN** I dug up on the island is still safely tucked away in my bag, when something catches my eye out the window. It's Mia, waving to me from next door. She signals for me to meet her outside.

Mia can't wait to show me the new unicorn video game characters she's drawn, inspired by my television appearance. They're so cool. I'm happy something good has come out of my **ORDEAL** at least! UNICORNFLICT is going to be more epic than Manic Mayhem Battle Battalion Shoot Squad IX – and that's saying something!

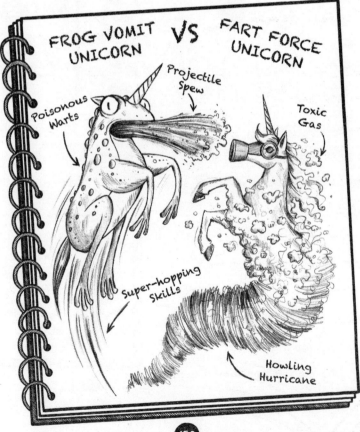

I fill Mia in on EVERYTHING that happened to me and she listens **intently**.

I think she would like to have a few words to Princess! It feels **GREAT** to talk about it all with a friend. Even as I hear myself recounting my adventures it sounds like a made-up children's story that couldn't possibly have happened.

Except I have this **TALISMAN** from the island as **proof!** I hold the strange artefact out to show Mia.

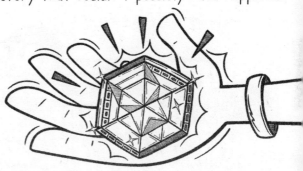

That's when Nickers snatches it from my hand and bounds off with the talisman in her jaws towards the cemetery.

I'm too **exhausted** to chase after her though. Whatever it was, it was probably **FAKE** anyway, just like the **PLASTIC** treasure in the island gift shop. Nickers can go **bury** it again for all I care! No big deal.

I realise I haven't called Mum yet. **SHE** (unlike Dad!) must be **worried** sick about me. I race inside to get my phone.

Marvin has his headphones on at his computer but I still tippy-toe across to my side of the bedroom. I can see he's editing **ANOTHER** video about me. Great! My bum getting even more **exposure**.

I call Mum's phone but she doesn't answer. Instead I'm greeted with a lifeless, MONOTONE, computer-generated voice.

YOU HAVE REACHED THE PHONE OF ANGELICA MARY-GRACE JOY MANALO DELA-CRUZ-STOKER, HOWEVER SHE IS UNABLE TO ATTEND YOUR CALL CURRENTLY.

I'm waiting for the **BEEP** to leave a message but there is only an impatient **SIGH**. I suddenly realise it's not a recording. It's actually Vlad!

Oh no. Talking on the phone is **painful** enough for me. Talking to my own stepfather/VAMPIRE is even more **EXCRUCIATING**.

Artist's impression only

'Um ... It's Justin.'

'I am well aware who you are.'

'Can I speak to Mum, please?'

'No.'

'Pretty please?' I try.

'Your mother is still recovering from her fainting episode this morning. She is in good health but following the doctor's orders of hydration and bed rest. I shall inform her of your call when she awakes from her slumber.'

And then he **HANGS UP** on me!

It's probably for the best that Mum slept through my KIDNAPPING. If she tracked me down to the Steel mansion I can only imagine the **BIG TROUBLE** everyone would be in!

I'm SHAKEN out of
my daydream by a familiar
NOISE at the window.
Could this be the return of
**CAPTAIN FLUFFYKINS?!**

I rush to the window
hoping to see **THIS.**

Instead I'm greeted with **THIS**.

A cluster of random **CATS**.

They stare directly at me with the same DISDAIN I'm used to from Captain Fluffykins. I try to **SHOO** them away but they don't even **flich**. They're really starting to **creep** me out! I back slowly away from the window and slam it shut.

I'm unsettled by the cat situation but there's no time to dwell on it. Final preparations for the **WEDDING** are in full swing now.

**5:35pm**

Dad, true to form, has gone with a **toilet-themed** wedding. I guess if Ms King has willingly agreed to this then it must actually be **REAL** love.

The spare lot next to our house has been converted into the wedding venue. Dad has constructed a STAGE for the ceremony, complete with a giant toilet-seat **archway**.

Mia is helping me put up the **decorations**. And by decorations I mean TOILET PAPER. Dad's bought in bulk!

The area Mia does looks like elegant PERFECTION.

The area I work on looks like someone has toilet-papered it as a cruel **Halloween** prank.

## 5:56pm

The special wedding **CAKE** is delivered by the chef.

## 6:09pm

Nan is still crocheting **madly,** putting the finishing touches on her mammoth project.

## 6:32pm

Dad is getting **GLAMMED** up. The **less** said about the spray tan the better.

Ms King is due back from the beauty salon any second. I better get dressed too. Guests will start arriving **soon.** This **wedding,** whether I like it or not, is about to happen.

6:58pm

Welcome
to the next
exciting
episode of:

EVENING
EDITION:
LIVE FROM
THE WEDDING
FRONTLINE

STARRING MISS DENISE AS <u>GOOD COP</u> AND MISS BERNICE AS <u>BAD COP</u>

**7:00pm**

Ms King makes her **SPECTACULAR** entrance in the wedding gown Nan has been crocheting all day. She looks like a life-sized TOILET ROLL DOLLLY!

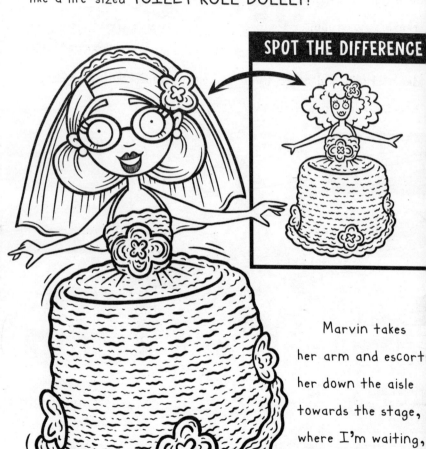

**SPOT THE DIFFERENCE**

Marvin takes her arm and escort her down the aisle towards the stage, where I'm waiting, as **Best Man**, alongside Dad.

160

As soon as he claps eyes on the bride, Dad starts **SPLUTTERING** and **SNIFFLING**. He's trying to hold back the **ugly tears**, but there's no stopping them!

I rip off a few sheets of the nearby toilet-paper decorations and offer them to Dad to wipe away his tears and blow his nose. Pretty **AND** practical!

With everyone in position, the ceremony can commence.

HONK!

Getting good use out of my wedding suit!

Miss Murmbles, substitute teacher and apparently part-time wedding celebrant, is here to officiate the proceedings. And to **GLARE** at me. No extra charge. Seems like she's still holding a **grudge** against me from Tuesday. Move on already!

I still can't properly hear or understand a word she is saying so I tune out. This talky-talk **blah blah blah** part of a wedding is always so **BORING**. Let's get to the cake!

I gradually become aware that everyone is **STARING** at me and I **SNAP** back to the moment and try to **focus** on what Miss Murmbles is saying.

That's my cue! I reach into my pocket and **suavely** pull out the ring box entrusted to me. BEST Best Man ever!

POP!

CHOMP!

WOOF!*

WOOF!

*Must have the Precious!

'NICKERS!

NOOOOOOOOO!'

I can't let Nickers run off with the rings. I'll be stripped of my **BEST MAN** title! I frantically chase the brazen dog **THIEF** all over and around the wedding.

JUSTIN LUCKY CHASE
BEST MAN
REVOKED
ONLY RESPONSIBILITY:
THE RINGS!

Sorry, Marvin!
(Not that sorry.)

Sorry, Mr Majors! (Again, not **THAT** sorry.)

CRUNCH!

Now I have Nickers **CORNERED!**

I **LUNGE** forward with a flying leap and manage to snatch the ringbox from Nickers' drooling jaws.

I also manage to land right in the WEDDING CAKE.

It's the second cake I've been inside today, which must be some kind of record! **Chocolate** mousse this time, which looks a bit SUSPICIOUS for a toilet cake. Tastes better than fruit cake at least!

More importantly though, the rings have been **SAVED** from a secret burial. The Best Man (ME!) has **triumphed!** The wedding can continue.

It's **OFFICIAL**. Here's the wedding photo to prove it.

That makes my school principal my **stepmum** and my arch nemesis my **brother**! Neither of us are happy about that!

**10:30pm**

The wedding celebrations have actually been **FUN** (after I washed and got changed out of my chocolate-coated suit!).

Dad has taken to the stage. I hope it's not **ANOTHER** speech. I don't think I could take anymore.

'Dearly beloved. I have a **surprise**! I would like to sing a song to my new wife. And I shall be joined by a special guest.'

And out from the stage rises T.H.E. **JUSTIN CHASE!** That guy knows how to make an entrance. The crowd/wedding guests go WILD as Justin begins singing his latest hit single 'Thump'.

He sounds so good and looks so **cool**. And then Dad joins in singing, serenading Step-Principal with a few self-penned verses. In contrast, **HE** does **not** sound good or look cool, but he is definitely **feeling** the lyrics.

How does he do it?

## THUMP
## additional lyrics
## by Harold Chase

You make my heart beat
Like a warm toilet seat
On a winter's day.
You feel so sweet!

You're surprising
Like a cool bidet
On a summer's day.
Heartbeat's rising!

167

As the song finishes, Dad leaps into his blushing bride's arms and I rush onto the stage. 'Justin! **WHAT** are you doing singing at my dad's wedding?!'

T.H.E. Justin Chase flashes his perfect, cheeky smile. 'I got to hang out with your old man for a while this morning when the TV studio was in lockdown.

Your dad's a good guy, and he's given me a new appreciation for toilets. Plus I'd do anything for my name buddy ... JUSTIN CHASE.' He holds out his fist.

**YES!** We get to do our **secret handshake** again.

We're mid squid fingers when the loud, **BUZZING** sound of helicopter blades pierces the air right above us.

Is it the paparazzi? Is it a news chopper? No, it's ...

That was quite an entrance, too. Princess picks herself up, **DAZED**, from the floor and readjusts her tiara.

'Ummm. Justin, meet Princess,' I say, fulfilling my end of the escape bargain. 'It's her birthday.'

'Happy birthday, Princess!' Justin sings sweetly.

Princess can't speak. Either she's **STARSTRUCK** or seeing stars from the impact of her **CRASH** landing. There's plenty of **drool** either way.

'Ummm. How about a quick group selfie, then I've gotta bail. I've still got more rehearsals and interviews to do,' T.H.E. Justin sighs as he slips away into the night.

Princess has regained the power of speech and is inspecting the photo. 'Nice! I can crop you right out, Poo Boy. Then I'll add a **filter**. I'm going to post this photo online **EVERYWHERE**. My **friends** are going to come crawling back OK. Gotta fly,' she says, as she hails her helicopter.

## REALITY ➡ ONLINE

THE_REAL_PRINCE$$

Just casually dropped in to see my bae. He sang me Happy Birthday. So cute.

I **really** need to go to the toilet. And it looks like everyone else at the wedding needs to as well! There's a long **queue** of guests going up the stairs, **WINCING** and MOANING, desperate to use the bathroom in our house.

I have my **SUSPICIONS!**

Dad insisted on serving his kale, cucumber and cabbage **SENSATION** cleansing **SMOOTHIE** as the special drink for the wedding **toasts.** Combine **THAT** with the wedding cake icing and all-you-can-eat buffet and I know only too well what that spells. **DISASTER** x 100 guests.

The queue is moving too slowly. I need a toilet **NOW**. I didn't want to have to resort to this, but I have no choice. Dad hired some **PORT-A-LOOS** that are lined up in the yard.

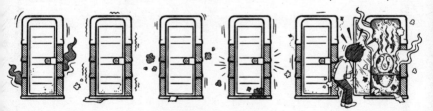

They're always so **GROSS** but I genuinely can't hold back the tide. I take a **gulp** of fresh air before entering the only vacant port-a-loo. What **HORRORS** await me?

# SCENE DELETED

## BY THE CENSORS

(SERIOUSLY, YOU DO NOT WANT TO SEE OR SMELL THIS.)

Please enjoy these awesome axolotl pictures instead ...

I burst out the port-a-loo door and **GASP** for clean air.
I couldn't do it. I just couldn't. My **germ phobia** kicked in
and I **CLENCHED** up. Maybe I can wait this out and use
the proper inside toilet. Everyone will be leaving soon. In
fact it looks like Dad and Step-Principal are leaving **NOW!**

They're making their way through the guard of honour
(technically guard of toilet plungers) towards the wedding
car (technically Dad's work toilet truck).

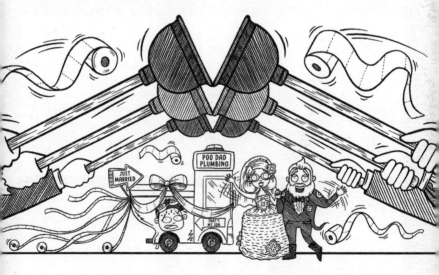

We're all waving goodbye when I realise I **cannot**
actually wait a millisecond longer. I **HAVE** to go into the
**PORT-A-LOO** and do what I have to do!

# SCENE DELETED

## BY THE CENSORS
(SERIOUSLY, DE JA POO.)

Please enjoy these sweet baby sloth pictures instead ...

I'm currently confined in my PUTRID port-a-loo prison, holding my breath and wearily weathering the **STORM** erupting from my buttocks, when I hear outside ...

... the **SCREECH** of tyres ...

... a loud metallic **BANG!** ...

... and then a ... **THUD! THUD! THUD!**

... getting louder and CLOSER. **THUD!**

The lights go out!

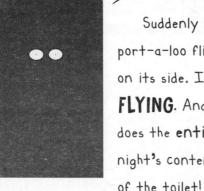

Suddenly the port-a-loo flips on its side. I go **FLYING**. And so does the **entire** night's contents of the toilet!

**SLOSH!**

176

# SCENE DELETED

## BY THE CENSORS

(SERIOUSLY, THIS TIME IT WENT TOO FAR,
EVEN BY WORST WEEK EVER STANDARDS.)

Please enjoy these fluffy round birdy pictures instead ...

The smell. The texture. The slimy squishiness. **EVERYWHERE!**

I push the door open and **clamber** out of the port-a-loo as fast as I possibly can, considering my pants are still down around my ankles.

And then I realise I have an audience. The whole remaining wedding party has rushed over to the toilet dominoes demolition site. They look on stunned and **AGHAST!** (Except Marvin! It's the happiest he's been all evening.)

I need some serious PIXELATION here. And some hospital-grade disinfectant. And a high-pressure water blaster. And, most urgently, a **new identity**. I quickly whip up my pants as the crowd forms a concerned circle around me.

I'm frozen in EMBARRASSMENT. Totally **MORTIFIED.**
Everyone is **staring.** I wish the ground would just
completely swallow me up.

And then it does.

And if you thought **THURSDAY** was thoroughly bad,
just wait until ...

# FUN FACTS

## WITH JUSTIN CHASE

Definitely **DO NOT** eat this frog – the **Golden Poison Frog** is the most **POISONOUS** animal in the world. While it is only the length of a paper clip, its vibrant-coloured skin secretes enough nerve **TOXIN** to kill 10 humans.

Fear of frogs and toads is called **RANIDAPHOBIA**.

The name **PIRANHA** comes from the indigenous Brazilian Tupi language and it means **TOOTH FISH**, but these fearsome fish rarely attack humans (except in movies and outlandish kids' books). Some piranhas are even vegetarian!

A **SPHINX** is a mythological creature with the body of a lion and the head of a human. In **Egypt,** the sphinx was often depicted with a Pharoah headdress whereas the **Greek** sphinx had eagle wings.

Pi is the ratio of the circumference to the diameter of a circle. Just in case you're ever on a quiz show and they ask what the value of **PI** to 12 decimal places is, the answer is $3.141592653589$.

**DOGS** aren't being gross when they sniff each other's **BUTTS** as a greeting. With their sensitive noses, **scents** in the glands around the rear-end can tell a dog about the gender, diet, health status and temperament of their new poochy pal.

# HOW TO DRAW:
# MIA

### STEP 1
Start with two circles for eyes.

### STEP 2
Draw a big circle around the smaller circles for her face.

### STEP 3
Do dots for the pupils and little curved lines for the nose and eyelashes.

### STEP 4
Draw the eyebrows and mouth next – these features determine her expression.

### STEP 5
Add in the ears and headband – they are just 'C' shapes.

### STEP 6
Then draw her hair – basically a big cloud with lots of bumps.

### STEP 7
For the finishing touch, colour in her hair and add some stray curls. (Mia is too busy designing Unicornflict to care about her hair that much!)

SHOCKED

SERIOUS

# WHAT'S <u>YOUR</u> PREDICTION FOR FRIDAY?

_____

_____

_____

_____

_____

_____

_____

Draw an illustration of Friday.

# ESCAPE SOLUTIONS

Upside down so you don't accidentally see the answers.

## COOL

The answer to the riddle is SNOW. You can make a snowball, it won't bounce but it will run away/melt when it's hot.

## S.O.S.

Dig at the letter X because X marks the spot. Part of the pirate rap in 'S.O.S.' (page 54 of Worst Week Ever: WEDNESDAY)

## MIRROR, MIRROR

When read in a reflection in the mirror the message is clear:

PUT YOUR HEAD DOWN AND FOLLOW YOUR HEART

PUT YOUR
HEAD DOWN
AND FOLLOW
YOUR HEART

## LET ME IN

Knock!
Knock!
Knock!

Re-enacting all the lyrics to 'LET ME IN' (page 64 of Worst Week Ever: MONDAY) releases the keys

## FACE 2 FACE

JUSTIN CHASE IS ACE

3 & 10 are identical

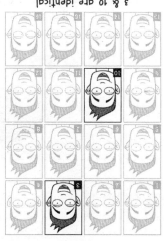

## MAZE

# AND NOW ... A BRIEF MESSAGE FROM

# EVA & MATT

SHE WROTE
THE WORDS

HE WROTE THE
OTHER WORDS
**AND** DREW THE
PICTURES

LITTLE
EVA:
Looking
very frilly

LITTLE
MATT:
Looking
very silly

Hey there _____ (Unless this is a library book. In that case,
YOUR NAME HERE  just imagine your name here. Or use invisible ink.)

YOU made it through THURSDAY. Congratulations! We already
suspected you were smart for choosing to read* WORST WEEK
EVER but this confirms you are a bonafide genius!

Have you ever been to a real escape room? Did you find it:

a) challenging?

b) rewarding?

c) surprising?

d) exhilarating?

e) all of the above?

*Assuming you are actually
reading the books and
not using them for a door
stop, squashing spiders,
weight lifting, jaunty hats
or toilet paper. YIKES!

We feel all of those things, and more, when we're writing WORST WEEK EVER. Creating each book is like putting together a puzzle for us. Mostly though it's just plain fun and makes us laugh. We hope the books make you laugh too!

As usual, lots of the funny situations in THURSDAY were inspired by things that have happened to us in real life. Just like Justin, we've worn some seriously bad fashion and had some very embarrassing moments freezing in the spotlight.

As a teenager, Eva was a super-fan (but definitely not a diva like Princess!) and 'accidentally' ended up ON stage with her favourite band. Meanwhile, Matt fell OFF stage during a play!

Anyway, we hope you NEVER have a week like Justin's and always manage to escape any room you don't want to be in! See you FRIDAY.

Best wishes,

*Eva ♡ Matt :)*

**P.S.** Can you do the secret Justin Chase handshake?!

**P.P.S.** Keep reading! The best way to try out lots of books is to be a member of your local library. Can you believe there are FREE books just waiting for you to borrow them? OK, so you do have to return them, but then you can borrow MORE free books! How amazing are libraries?! Answer: REALLY amazing!

**P.P.P.S.** Be careful what you wish for!

**EVA AMORES** is a designer/photographer who has worked for the Sydney Opera House and the ABC. She was born in the Philippines and moved to Australia during high school. She likes shoes, travelling and more shoes.

**MATT COSGROVE** is the best-selling author/illustrator of *Macca the Alpaca* and the *Epic Fail Tales* series. He was born and raised in Western Sydney. He likes chocolate, avoiding social interactions and more chocolate.

Eva and Matt met when they were randomly placed together for a group assignment at university twenty-five years ago and they've been collaborating ever since. They've made dinner, cakes, a mess, the bed, mistakes, memories, poor fashion decisions and two actual humans, but this is their first book series together.

When they were in lockdown and the world felt a bit grim, they could have mastered sourdough or binge watched Netflix but, no, they decided to create this series instead – THE WORST WEEK EVER! (Sorry about that.)

WITH GLASSES
(in case they're in disguise)

Here's a photo of Eva and Matt so if you ever see them in real life you know to run in the opposite direction.